LITTLE WOMEN

LITTLE WOMEN

Adapted by Fiona Patchett

from the story by Louisa May Alcott

Illustrated by Sophie Allsopp

CONTENTS

1. A Christmas Letter   7

2. Merry Christmas!   14

3. The Laurence Boy   20

4. Mother's Sermon   27

5. Making Friends   34

6. Beth's Palace   41

7. Amy's Shame   47

8. Jo's Anger   52

9. Meg's Vanity   58

10. The Pickwick Club   65

11. An Experiment   70

12. Camp Laurence   77

13. Castles in the Air 86

14. Secrets 92

15. A Telegram 100

16. Mother Leaves 107

17. Faithful Little Beth 111

18. Dark Days 116

19. Amy's Will 122

20. Confiding in Mother 130

21. Laurie Makes Mischief 136

22. Pleasant Days 145

23. Aunt March Settles the Question 152

CHAPTER ONE

A Christmas Letter

"Christmas won't be Christmas without any presents," grumbled Jo March.

"I hate being poor!" said Meg, her sister.

"I don't think it's fair that some girls have lots of pretty things and others nothing at all," sighed Amy, the youngest.

"At least we have Father, Mother and each other," Beth said contentedly.

"But we haven't got Father and we won't have for a long time," said Jo. She didn't say *perhaps never*, but each sister added it silently, thinking of their father away at war.

"Mother said we shouldn't spend our money on presents for ourselves when there are men suffering in the army," Meg reminded them.

"But a dollar each isn't enough to help the army," said Jo. "I'll buy a book with mine."

"I'll spend mine on new music," said Beth.

"I'll buy drawing pencils," decided Amy.

"We work hard enough to earn it," Jo added.

"I know I do, teaching those horrible King children," began Meg.

"Huh. How would you like to look after fussy old Aunt March and her parrot?" asked Jo.

"Washing dishes makes my hands so stiff, I can't play the piano," said Beth, with a sigh.

"None of you suffer like I do," cried Amy, "when the girls at school laugh at my old, patched dresses."

"I know!" said Beth. "Let's each get a present for Mother, instead of for ourselves."

"What will we get?" exclaimed Jo.

"A nice pair of gloves," Meg announced.

"A pretty handkerchief," said Beth.

"New slippers from me!" cried Jo.

"I'll get her a little bottle of perfume," added Amy, "then I'll have enough left to buy something for myself."

"Let Mother think we are getting things for ourselves and then we'll surprise her," said Jo. "We'll go shopping tomorrow."

"I'm glad to find you girls so merry," said a cheery voice at the door. Mother was home.

"Marmee!" chorused the girls.

"Sorry I'm late," Mrs. March went on, "but I have a treat for you all after supper."

A smile went around the girls like a streak of sunshine and Jo cried, "A letter from Father!"

"Yes, a nice long letter. He is well and sends his love," said Mrs. March, patting her pocket as if she had a treasure there.

"When will he come home, Marmee?" asked Beth, with a little quiver in her voice.

"Not for many months. He has work to do and we won't ask for him back any sooner."

After supper, they sat around the fire as Mother read the letter. It was lively and full of hope. At the very end, he wrote:

A year seems a long time before I see them again, but I know they will be loving children and work hard to improve their characters, so that when I come back, I will be prouder than ever of my little women.

Everybody sniffed when they came to that part. Jo wasn't ashamed of the great tear that dropped off the end of her nose, and Amy sobbed, "I know I can be selfish! But I'll try to be better, so he won't be disappointed in me."

"We all will," cried Meg. "I think about my looks too much and hate to work, but I will try to improve."

"I'll try to be *a little woman* and not be so rough and wild," said Jo.

Beth wiped away her tears and quietly resolved to be everything Father hoped she would be when he came home.

"Look under your pillows on Christmas morning," said Mother. "You will each find a little book that will help guide you."

CHAPTER TWO

Merer Christmas!

Jo was the first to wake on Christmas morning. No stockings hung at the fireplace and, for a moment, she felt disappointed. Then she remembered what Mother had said, slipped her hand under her pillow and pulled out a crimson book. Inside, a few words written by Mother made it even more precious. When Meg, Beth and Amy woke, they found their little books too – one green, one brown and one blue.

"I shall keep mine by my bed and read a little every morning," said Meg.

"I'm glad mine is blue," said Amy. Then the room went very still while all the girls softly turned the pages.

"Where is Mother?" asked Meg eventually, as she and Jo ran down to thank her.

"Some poor person needed help. I've never known anyone help those in need like your mother," replied Hannah, their housekeeper.

"She'll be back soon," said Meg, looking at their presents for Mother in a basket.

"Here she is now. Hide the basket, quick!" cried Jo, as they heard footsteps in the hall.

It was Amy.

"Where have you been?" asked Meg.

"Don't laugh!" she said. "I didn't want

anyone to know. I ran to the shop and changed the little bottle of perfume for a big one. I'm trying not to be so selfish, after reading about being good in my book."

There was another bang at the door. This time it *was* Mother.

"Merry Christmas, Marmee! Thank you for our books. We've read some already," they said as they all hurried to the table for breakfast.

"Merry Christmas!" she said. "Now, I want to say one word before we start. Not far from here live the Hummel family, and they are very cold and hungry. Girls, will you give them your breakfast as a Christmas present?"

For a minute, no one spoke. Then Jo cried, "I'm so glad you told us before we began!"

"I knew you'd do it," said Mrs. March.

Soon they were ready to set off.

They found a poor, bare room, with broken windows, no fire, a sick mother, a wailing baby and a group of hungry children huddled under one old quilt, trying to keep warm.

"Angels have come!" gasped Mrs. Hummel, crying for joy as they arrived.

"Funny angels in hoods and mittens," said Jo, making them laugh.

The girls sat the children around the fire and fed them like hungry birds. It was a very happy breakfast, even though they didn't get to eat any of it.

Once they were home, Mrs. March opened her presents. The slippers went on at once; the new handkerchief was slipped into her pocket; she was well-scented with Amy's perfume; and the gloves were declared a perfect fit.

Later that day, they performed a play Jo had

written, before Hannah called them for supper.
The feast took their breath away. There was
cake, fruit, pink *and* white ice cream, French
bonbons and four huge bunches of flowers.

"Did the fairies bring it?" asked Amy.

"Santa Claus," said Beth.

"Mother did it," suggested Meg.

"Aunt March felt generous for a change!"
cried Jo, with sudden inspiration.

"All wrong. Old Mr. Laurence next door sent
it," replied Mrs. March. "Hannah told him
about your kindness this morning."

"But he doesn't know us!" said Meg.

"His grandson looks as though he wants to
be our friend," said Jo. "But he's always
studying. I expect he put the idea into his
grandfather's head. I mean to get to know him.
I think he needs some fun."

CHAPTER THREE

The Laurence Boy

"Jo! Jo! Look! An invitation for a New Year's Eve dance tomorrow!" called Meg, waving the precious paper with delight. "Marmee says we can go. Now what *shall* we wear? If only I had a silk dress and better gloves."

"My party dress is scorched where I stood too close to the fire *and* my gloves have lemonade all over them," said Jo, who was not interested in clothes in the least.

"We can each wear one of my good gloves and hold one of yours," decided Meg.

New Year's Eve came and the two elder girls were getting ready. Meg wanted a few curls, so Jo took a pair of hot tongs to her hair.

"Should it smoke like that?" asked Beth.

"It smells like burned feathers," observed Amy, smoothing her own golden curls.

The horrified hairdresser watched as singed locks fell onto the victim's lap.

"Oh, oh! What have you done?" wailed Meg. "I can't go now! My poor hair!"

"Just tie it in ribbons and it will look like the latest fashion. I've seen many girls do it," said Amy, consoling her.

Finally, they were ready to go – Meg in blue velvet and lace and Jo in red, with a gentlemanly white collar.

The sisters were not used to big parties and hung back, feeling shy. A stately old lady greeted them and introduced them to her daughters. One of the boys asked Meg to dance at once, but Jo felt so out of place that she slipped behind a curtain, so she could watch the dancing unseen. To her surprise, another bashful person was there already. She found herself face to face with the Laurence boy.

"I didn't know anyone was here!" she stammered.

But the boy said pleasantly, "Don't mind me. Stay if you like. My name's Laurie."

"I'm Jo. Don't you live near us?"

"Next door." He looked up and laughed, his eyes shining with fun, putting Jo at ease.

"We did enjoy your nice Christmas present."

"Grandpa sent it," he replied. They talked for ages, finding out about each other. Then Laurie

asked, "Do you like to dance?"

"Only if there's plenty of room. In a place like this, it's too easy to tread on people's toes or do something else dreadful," Jo said.

"There's a long hall out there, where no one will get in our way. Let's try this polka!"

Laurie taught her the steps and they whirled up and down the hall. As the music stopped, they sat down to catch their breath. Laurie had begun to tell Jo about his travels when Meg appeared, limping.

"I've sprained my ankle in those stupid, tight shoes. I don't know how I'll get home."

When Hannah arrived to accompany them home, Meg got up so quickly, she cried in pain.

"Please let me take you," said Laurie, offering his grandfather's carriage.

So they all rolled home in old Mr. Laurence's luxurious carriage. Laurie went at the front

with Hannah and the girls sat in the back, where they could talk about the party without being overheard.

"I had an excellent time. Did you?" asked Jo.

"Oh yes," Meg nodded. "Until I hurt myself. But what were you and Laurie doing all that time, hidden away?"

By the time Jo had finished telling her about Laurie, they were home. They crept in, hoping not to disturb anyone. But the instant their door creaked, two sleepy voices called, "Tell about the party! Tell about the party!"

"I don't believe anyone could have enjoyed themselves more than we did," declared Jo, "even with burned hair, old dresses, one glove each and tight shoes!"

CHAPTER FOUR

Mother's Sermon

"How hard it seems to go on with daily life," sighed Meg, the morning after the party. "I envy girls who go to parties all the time. It's not fair that we have to work!"

Meg was not the only grumpy one that morning. Beth had a headache, Amy was working hard at her schoolwork and Jo was making a racket getting ready for work.

Mrs. March was trying to finish a letter and Hannah was sleepy from staying up so late.

When Meg, Jo and Amy set out into the wind, their smiling Mother waved to them from the window, as she always did.

Beth was too shy to go to school, so she did her lessons at home and helped Hannah. She was not lonely because she had three kittens and six broken dolls to look after. The shabbiest doll of all was Joanna, but she was the most loved. Beth adored music and tried hard to play the old out-of-tune piano.

"I'll get a better piano one day, if I'm good," she said to herself.

That evening, as they all sat together sewing, Meg said, "Has anybody got anything to tell? I'm dying for some amusement."

"I was reading such a dull book to Aunt

March today," began Jo, who loved to tell stories. "I yawned so wide, she said I could swallow the book whole! Then she snapped, *I don't understand what that book is about. Begin it again, child.* Her life would be so much nicer if she chose to be kind! I don't envy her at all, in spite of her money."

"That reminds me," said Meg, "one of the King children said her brother had done something shameful. Then I heard Mrs. King crying. I didn't ask any questions, but I felt so sorry for them, however rich they are."

"Susie Perkins came to school today," said Amy, "with a lovely red ring. I envied her dreadfully. Well, she drew a picture of Mr. Davis, with a monstrous nose and the words *Young ladies, I'm watching you!* coming out of his mouth. We were laughing away, until all of a sudden he *was* watching us! He ordered Susie to stand at the front of the class and hold up the picture so everyone could see it. I didn't envy her then, for all the pretty rings in the world."

"When I went to get some oysters this morning," Beth began, "a poor woman came into the shop and asked the fishmonger if she could do some cleaning for a bit of fish, because she had no food for her children. He said *No!* rather crossly. Old Mr. Laurence was in the shop. He picked up a whole fish and gave it to her. Wasn't that kind? She did look funny, hugging the big, slippery fish!"

When they had laughed at Beth's story, they asked their mother for one.

"Once upon a time," said Mrs. March, "there were four girls, who had enough to eat

and drink, kind friends and parents who loved them, and yet they were not content. So they asked an old woman for a spell to make them happy. She simply said, *Count your blessings and be grateful.* Being sensible girls, they took her advice. One discovered that even though she was poor, she was kind, unlike a certain old lady; the second that money couldn't keep shame out of rich people's lives; the third that even expensive rings are not as valuable as behaving well; and the fourth that, however hard she had to work, it was not as hard as begging for food. They all agreed to stop complaining and enjoy the blessings they already had."

"Marmee, you are clever to turn our stories into a sermon!" cried Meg. "We needed that lesson and we won't forget it."

CHAPTER FIVE

Making Friends

"What in the world are you doing now, Jo?" asked Meg, one snowy afternoon, when her sister appeared with a broom in one hand and a shovel in the other.

"Going out in the snow," said Jo, with a mischievous twinkle in her eyes.

"Stay warm by the fire like I do," said Meg.

"Cats curl up and doze all day by the fire.

I like adventures and I'm going to find some."

Jo went out and started digging paths in the snow. A low hedge separated the March's plain but snug home from old Mr. Laurence's grand mansion next door. For all its magnificence, it seemed a lifeless sort of place to Jo. She longed to discover the hidden glories inside. And since the party, she was more eager than ever to get to know the Laurence boy.

Just then, she spied his face at an upper window. "Poor boy! All alone," she thought, tossing up a handful of snow. His head turned.

"How are you? Are you sick?" she called.

Laurie opened the window and croaked, "Better, thank you. I've had a cold all week. It's so dull up here with no one to talk to."

"I could come over and amuse you," said Jo. "Just let me ask Mother."

Laurie was in a flutter of nerves at the thought of having a visitor. But when Jo arrived, with Beth's kittens in her arms – "Beth thought they might be comforting!" said Jo – he forgot his shyness immediately.

"Beth is the rosy one, I believe. Is Meg the older one and Amy the curly-haired one?"

"How did you find that out?" asked Jo.

Laurie blushed. "I often hear you calling to one another. When the lamps are lit, it's like looking at a picture to see you all around the table with your mother. I haven't got a mother, you know."

Jo was touched by the sadness in his voice.

"Come over. We'll make you laugh," she said, and Laurie's face brightened at once.

The pair talked and talked. Jo found out that Laurie loved books as much as she did.

"Would you like to see our books? Grandpa is out, so you needn't be afraid," he said.

"I'm not afraid of anything!" retorted Jo.

The library was lined with books and stuffed with ornaments and portraits.

Just then, a bell rang and Jo exclaimed with alarm, "It's your grandpa!"

"What if it is? You're not afraid of anything," replied Laurie, looking wicked.

"The doctor to see you, Sir," said the maid.

While Laurie was out of the room, Jo was admiring a portrait of old Mr. Laurence, when the door opened. Without turning, she said, "I wouldn't be afraid of him. He's got kind eyes, even if his mouth is grim."

"So you're not afraid of me, hey?" said a gruff voice behind her. There, to her horror, stood old Mr. Laurence.

"Not much, Sir," said Jo, blushing scarlet.

"You've certainly got your grandfather's spirit. I remember him well. He was a fine gentleman," he said.

"Thank you, Sir," said Jo.

"What have you been doing to this boy of mine?" was his next question.

"Making friends. I thought he must be lonely, here on his own," she replied.

Laurie came back in, and the old gentleman noticed new life in his grandson's face. He looked pleased.

"You must come and visit us again, Dr. Jo," he said. "Your medicine seems to be working wonders."

CHAPTER SIX

Beth's Palace

The friendship between Laurie and the March girls flourished. What good times they had: plays, sleigh rides, ice skating, snug evenings and merry parties. The Laurence house seemed like a palace to Jo, Meg and Amy. But shy Beth could not pluck up the courage to visit, even when she learned there was a grand piano in the drawing room.

Old Mr. Laurence heard about her love of music and one afternoon, when he was visiting Mrs. March, he casually mentioned the piano. Silently Beth crept nearer, her eyes wide with excitement.

"Our piano needs someone to use it," he said. "Would some of your girls like to come over and play it, just to keep it in tune?"

Beth took another step forward.

"They needn't see or speak to anyone," he went on. "I'm usually in my study and Laurie is often out. Of course, if they don't care to come, never mind."

Beth looked up at him and said earnestly, "Oh Sir, they do care, very, very much!"

"Are you the musical girl?" he asked.

"I'm Beth and I love music dearly. I'll come, if you are sure nobody will hear me," she added, trembling at her own boldness.

"Not a soul, my dear. So please play as much as you like. I shall be obliged to you."

"How kind you are, Sir!"

The next day, she made her way as quietly as a mouse, through the hedge, in at the side door of the great mansion and into the drawing room. As soon as she touched the piano keys, she forgot her fear, only feeling the pure delight which the music gave her.

After that, she played nearly every day. She never knew that Mr. Laurence opened his study door so he could hear her, or that Laurie asked the servants to be quiet.

Beth sewed Mr. Laurence a pair of slippers to thank him, and when they were finished, Laurie delivered them.

One day, she came home to see her sisters

at the window, waving a letter.

"It's from the old gentleman! Quick, let's read it!" cried their joyful voices.

Beth turned pale with delight and surprise, for there stood a piano, with a letter on the lid to Miss Elizabeth March.

"You read it! I can't! It's too lovely!" she said to Jo.

Jo began to laugh, for the first words she read were: "*Dear Madame—*"

"How elegant it sounds!" said Amy.

"*I have never had a pair of slippers that suited me so well,*" continued Jo. "*Please allow me to send you this gift. Your grateful and humble friend, James Laurence.*"

"Try it, honey," said Hannah, who always shared in the family's joys and sorrows.

So Beth lovingly began to play. Then, to the

amazement of her family, she said, "I'm going to thank him."

She walked straight into the Laurence house and right up to Mr. Laurence. With only a small quaver in her voice, she said, "I came to thank you, Sir, for…" But he looked so friendly that she forgot her speech, put both arms around his neck and hugged him. And together they talked as if she had known him all her life.

He walked her home, with Beth chatting merrily beside him, to the astonishment of her watching sisters.

Jo danced a jig, Amy nearly fell out of the window in surprise, and Meg threw up her hands and exclaimed, "Well! I do believe the world is coming to an end!"

CHAPTER SEVEN

Amy's Shame

"I wish I had some money," sobbed Amy, one morning.

"Why?" asked Meg.

"I owe at least a dozen pickled limes to the girls at school," she replied.

"Are limes the fashion now? It used to be bits of rubber to make balls," said Meg.

"It's nothing but limes now. Everyone is

eating them, or trading them for pencils or paper dolls. I've eaten plenty, but now I have to pay them back."

"How much do you need?" asked Meg.

"A quarter would do it," said Amy, as Meg opened her purse.

Limes were forbidden in class, but Amy could not resist proudly displaying her brown paper bag in front of her classmates, before stashing it away in her desk. Within minutes, everyone was whispering that Amy March had twenty-four delicious limes and was planning to treat her friends.

Jenny Snow offered to give her the answers to some difficult sums. But Jenny had made a mean comment when Amy had no limes, so Amy instantly crushed her hopes with the words, "You needn't be so polite all of a sudden, for you won't get any of mine."

Furious, Jenny told the teacher, Mr. Davis, that Amy had some limes in her desk.

"Miss March, bring your limes to the front," he boomed.

"Don't take them all," whispered a quick-thinking friend.

Amy shook out half a dozen and took the others, certain that Mr. Davis would soften when he smelled their delicious scent. Unfortunately, Mr. Davis hated limes.

"Is that all? Bring the rest," he demanded.

Reluctantly, Amy obeyed.

"Now stand at the front until break," he barked at her.

Amy suffered a sense of shame she never forgot. Worst of all was knowing that her family would be so disappointed in her.

At break, she snatched up her things and, without a word to anyone, she left.

"That school is full of unruly girls and I don't approve of the way Mr. Davis teaches," said Mrs. March. "I won't send you back there. You can study here with Beth."

"Good! I wish all the girls would leave his silly old school. Think of all those lovely limes wasted," sighed Amy.

"You broke the rules and you deserved to lose them," was the severe reply. "You are becoming too self-important, my dear. You have many talents, but it is much more charming to be modest."

"I see," said Amy, thoughtfully. "So it is good to have talents and be elegant, but not to show off. I'll do better from now on, Marmee, I promise."

CHAPTER EIGHT

Jo's Anger

"Where are you going?" asked Amy, as Jo and Meg were getting ready to go out one Saturday afternoon.

"Little girls shouldn't ask questions," replied Jo, in a sharp tone that made Amy even more determined to find out.

Then she saw Meg slip a fan into her pocket and cried, "I know! You're going to see a play with Laurie! I'll come with you!"

"If she goes, I won't!" cried Jo. "A fidgety child will spoil all our fun."

Laurie arrived and the two older girls hurried downstairs.

"You'll be sorry for this, Jo March," Amy wailed over the bannister, as they left.

The play was wonderful, with comical imps and sparkling elves. But the golden curls of the fairy queen reminded Jo of Amy, and she began wondering what her sister would do to make her sorry.

The next day, Meg, Beth and Amy were sitting together, when Jo burst in, crying, "Has anyone taken my notebook?"

Meg and Beth said, "No," at once, but Amy poked the fire and said nothing.

"Amy, you've got it! And if you don't tell

me, I'll make you," she threatened.

"You'll never see it again," said Amy, "because I burned it!"

"What! The stories I was so fond of and meant to finish before Father came home? The stories I can never write again?" said Jo, turning very pale.

"I told you I'd make you pay for being so mean yesterday."

When Mrs. March heard the row, she explained to Amy that Jo had worked hard writing six fairy tales, hoping they'd be good enough to print. Now Amy deeply regretted what she'd done.

"Please forgive me, Jo," she said meekly.

"I will never forgive you!" roared Jo.

The following day, Jo was still in a rage. "I'm going skating with Laurie," she huffed.

"At least *he* is always kind."

"Go after her while she's with Laurie," Meg said to Amy, "Laurie is so kind, I'm sure she'll forgive you then."

Amy picked up her skates and ran after them. Laurie was skating far ahead along the river and didn't see Amy.

"Keep to the edge!" he called back to Jo. "The ice is too thin in the middle."

Amy didn't catch a word. Jo saw Amy putting on her skates, but didn't bother to tell her. "She can take care of herself," she thought, as she skated off after Laurie.

Even when she heard Amy heading straight for the middle, she still didn't warn her. Then something made her turn, just in time to see Amy crash through the ice. For a moment, her heart stood still with fear.

Laurie raced over, calling, "Quick! Help!"

She did all she could to help Laurie drag Amy out. Shivering, dripping and crying, they got her home, where she fell asleep, wrapped in blankets by a hot fire.

"You were so sensible getting her home quickly," Mother whispered to Jo.

"Laurie did it all. If she had drowned, it would have been my fault," sobbed Jo. "All because I lost my temper! I try to control it, Marmee, but sometimes I can't."

"Keep trying, my dear," soothed Mrs. March, "and you will. Try not to let the sun go down on your anger."

Jo leaned over and stroked Amy's golden hair. Amy woke and held out her arms to Jo, and all was forgiven in one warm hug.

CHAPTER NINE

Meg's Vanity

"I wish you could all come with me," said Meg, as her sisters helped her pack. She was going to stay for a week with her friend, Sallie Moffat, who was having a party.

"What did Mother give you from the treasure chest?" asked Amy.

"A pair of silk stockings and a blue sash, to go with my white ball dress," said Meg.

"You will look like an angel," said Amy.

"The dress is only cotton, not silk like Sallie's, but it will have to do," sighed Meg.

"You said the other day just going to Sallie's would make you happy," said Beth.

"So I did! But it seems as if the more one gets, the more one wants," said Meg.

The Moffats were fashionable and at first, Meg was daunted by the opulence of it all. Sallie's friends were elegant too, and Meg soon began to copy their airs and graces.

"What will you wear to the party?" asked Sallie. Meg pulled out her white dress but it looked shabby beside Sallie's crisp new dress. Meg saw the girls glance at each other and their pity made her heart ache.

Then, later, she overheard a conversation.

"No doubt her mother has plans for her to

marry the Laurence boy," said one voice.

"If only she was more stylish," replied Mrs. Moffat. "Do you think she'd mind if we lent her a better dress for the party?"

Meg tried to forget it, but that night in bed, hot tears ran down her cheeks.

On the day of the party, Sallie said, "Please let me dress you up. You'd be a real beauty with a touch here and there."

Meg wanted to see if she *would* be a *real beauty*, so she let Sallie crimp her hair, dust her neck with fragrant powder, paint her lips red and lace her into a blue silk dress, so tight she could hardly breathe. Silver bracelets, necklace and earrings were added, along with a feather fan. Sallie admired her like a little girl with a newly dressed doll.

Everyone at the party admired Meg. Then

she spotted Laurie. "I'm glad you came," she said. "The girls dressed me up for fun. I like it, don't you?"

"No, I don't," was the blunt reply.

"Why not?" she asked anxiously.

"I don't like fuss and feathers."

Meg walked off in a huff. Then she overheard someone else.

"They're making a fool of that girl. She's nothing but a doll tonight," said the voice.

"Oh dear!" thought Meg. "I wish I'd been sensible and worn my own things."

When she saw Laurie again, he bowed and said, "Please forgive me. I don't like your dress, but I think that you are splendid."

Friends again, they went twirling merrily around the dance floor. For the rest of the evening, Meg danced, flirted, chattered and

sipped champagne, just like the other girls.

"I'm not Meg tonight," she said to Laurie. "I'm a *doll* who does all sorts of crazy things. Tomorrow I'll be myself again."

The next day, she was relieved to get home.

"I had a wonderful time," she told her mother. "But they dressed me up like a doll and said I was a beauty, so I let them."

Then she told the gossip she had heard. "Marmee, do you have *plans* for us?"

"My only plan is for all my girls to live useful and pleasant lives. And if you do marry, only marry for love."

"I did enjoy being admired though," confessed Meg.

"That is perfectly natural," replied Mother. "But you must learn to know when the praise is worth having."

CHAPTER TEN

The Pickwick Club

When spring came, the girls amused themselves with walks, rowing on the river and flower hunts. Secret societies were the fashion and they had their own, called the Pickwick Club, or the P.C. for short. Each sister contributed to *The Pickwick Portfolio*, their weekly newspaper, and met every Saturday in the attic. Meg, as the eldest, was the president, and read the paper aloud.

It was filled with original tales, poetry, news, funny advertisements and hints, in which the girls made fun of each other. As Meg finished reading, Jo rose to speak.

"President and ladies," she began, "I wish to propose a new member to the club – one who would add to the literary value of the paper and also be jolly and nice. I propose Mr. Theodore Laurence."

Jo's formal tone made the girls laugh, but they also looked rather anxious.

"We'll put it to a vote," said the president. "All in agreement, please say *Aye*."

There was a loud response from Jo, followed by a timid one from Beth.

"Those against say *No*."

Meg and Amy said *No*. Amy rose and spoke with great dignity, "We do not wish to admit

any boys. This is a ladies' club and we would like it to remain private."

"I'm afraid he'll laugh at our paper and make fun of us," observed Meg.

Up rose Jo. "I give you my word, Laurie won't do anything of the sort. I think the least we can do is to make him welcome, after all he has done for us."

"I say he *may* join," said Beth, "And his grandpa too, if he likes."

This spirited outburst electrified the club.

"Now then, vote again," cried Jo excitedly.

"Aye! Aye! Aye!" replied all three voices.

"Good! Allow me to present the new member." To the dismay of the others, Jo threw open the cupboard door and there was Laurie, twinkling with laughter.

"Jo, how could you?" cried the three girls.

The new member spoke, "President and ladies – I planned all this, so please don't blame Jo. As a token of my thanks, I have set up a post office in the hedge. It is a sturdy box with padlocks on it, and will hold letters, books and bundles. Allow me to present the club key."

Then this unusually lively meeting broke up with three cheers for the new member.

No one ever regretted allowing Laurie to join the P.C. The old gentleman joined in the fun too, sending amusing messages and telegrams. His gardener even sent Hannah a love letter. How they laughed when this secret came out, never dreaming how many more love letters that little post office would hold in the years to come.

CHAPTER ELEVEN

An Experiment

"The King family are away. I have three weeks of freedom!" exclaimed Meg.

"Aunt March has gone away too," said Jo. "I was afraid she'd ask me to go with her!"

"Aunt March is a regular samphire, isn't she?" observed Amy.

"*Vampire*, not samphire," corrected Jo.

"What will you do with your time off?"

asked Amy, ignoring Jo's correction.

"I've spent all winter working for other people, so now I shall rest," replied Meg.

"I've a heap of books to read," said Jo, "when I'm not having lar—"

"Don't say *larks*! It's slang," said Amy, getting back at Jo. "Beth, let's rest and play too, instead of doing our lessons."

"May we, Mother?" asked Beth.

"Try it as an experiment and see how you like not working for a week," she replied.

The next day, no dusting or cleaning got done. Meg sat in the rocking chair, daydreaming about the pretty summer dresses she was planning to buy. Jo spent the morning reading. Beth began by clearing out her dolls' house, but tiring of that, she went to the piano. Amy put on her best white dress and went outside to draw under the honeysuckle, hoping someone would inquire who the young artist was. As no one appeared but a curious daddy-longlegs, she went for a walk and got caught in a shower.

By supper, they all agreed that it had been a delightful though unusually long day. They assured Mother that the experiment was working. She smiled and continued to help Hannah do their neglected housework.

On Saturday, Mrs. March went out for the day and gave Hannah a day off, so the girls could see the full effect of the experiment.

Jo invited Laurie for lunch. On her way to the kitchen, she found Beth sobbing over Pip, her canary, who had died.

"It's my fault, I forgot to feed him! Oh Pip, how could I be so cruel to you?" cried Beth.

"Don't cry, Bethy. Nothing has gone right this week," consoled Jo.

Jo did her best to make lunch. She boiled the asparagus until the heads came off, burned the bread black, then bashed the lobster to remove the shell, until there was hardly any left to eat. The strawberries were not ripe and the blancmange was lumpy.

Hot and tired, she called everyone for lunch. They tasted it, then left most of it. At least she had remembered to add plenty of sugar and cream to the strawberries. She handed around the dishes, going without herself, so there would be enough.

The corners of Laurie's mouth puckered. Then Amy choked and left the table.

"What is it?" exclaimed Jo, trembling.

"Salt instead of sugar and the cream is

sour," replied Meg, sympathetically.

Jo was on the verge of crying, when her eyes met Laurie's. The funny side struck her and they burst out laughing.

Mrs. March came home to find the girls busy clearing up.

"What a dreadful day it's been!" began Jo.

"Not a bit like home," added Amy.

"It can't be without Marmee and little Pip," sighed Beth.

"Would you like another week of the experiment?" asked Mother.

"No!" they all cried.

"Don't you feel that each doing your share makes play sweeter when it comes?"

"We do, Mother, we do!" cried the girls.

CHAPTER TWELVE

Camp Laurence

Beth loved her daily task of unlocking the little post office and distributing the mail to her family. One July day, she came in with a bundle of letters. Jo opened her letter, preparing herself for good or bad news. When she saw the small, neat handwriting, she knew it was from Laurie and began to read aloud...

Dear Jo,

Some English friends are coming to visit tomorrow. I'm going to row the whole crew up to Longmeadow for lunch, croquet and all sorts of larks. My tutor, Mr. Brooke, is coming and I want you all to come.

Yours ever, Laurie

"Will you come with us, Bethy?" asked Jo.

"As long as you'll take care of me."

"Good girl. Let's all work doubly hard today, so we can enjoy tomorrow," said Jo.

The next morning, bright sunshine streamed through the windows.

"There's Laurie," said Beth, looking out. "He's with a tall girl, a little girl and two dreadful boys. One of them has a crutch."

"And there's Sallie and Ned Moffat," cried Meg. "Oh, Jo, you're not going to wear that awful hat, are you? You look like a boy!"

"I don't mind looking like a boy if I'm comfortable," said Jo, as they trooped out.

Laurie introduced the March girls to his English friends. Amy quickly became friends with Grace, the little girl. Beth glanced at the boys, Fred and Frank. She felt sorry for Frank, the one with the crutch, so she decided she would at least be kind to him.

The two boats pushed off together. Meg was seated facing Mr. Brooke and Ned, who each tried to impress her with their rowing skills. She liked Mr. Brooke's quiet manners and knowledge about all things.

"Welcome to Camp Laurence!" said Laurie, as they reached Longmeadow. "Now let's play croquet before it gets too hot."

Mr. Brooke chose Meg, Fred and Kate, the tall English girl, for his team. Laurie took Jo,

Sallie and Ned. It was a close game. Fred's ball hit the last wicket, but stopped just an inch on the wrong side. No one was nearby, so he gave it a sly nudge with his toe.

"I'm through!" he cried.

"You pushed it. I saw you," said Jo.

"It rolled a bit, but that's allowed," he replied, croqueting her ball far away.

Jo opened her lips to say something rude, but instead went off to get her ball. After a long time finding it in the bushes, she came back, cool and calm. Then with one nimble stroke, she won the game.

Meg whispered to Jo, "I'm so glad you kept your temper."

"Don't praise me, Meg. I could scream at Fred this very minute," she replied.

Laurie announced lunch and they all sat

down to an inviting array of food and drinks, laid out on a tablecloth in the shade.

"There's salt here," Laurie said, as he handed Jo a saucer of berries.

"Thank you, but I prefer insects," she replied, as ants crawled all over them. "How dare you remind me of that horrid lunch!"

Meg and Mr. Brooke were sitting together.

"Do you know German?" he asked, laying his German book on her lap with a smile.

"A little," said Meg. "Father was teaching me, but now he's away." She read slowly and timidly, but her soft, musical voice made the difficult words sound like poetry.

"Very well read indeed!" said Mr. Brooke, ignoring her many mistakes.

"What will you do when Laurie goes to college next year?" she asked him.

"I shall become a soldier," he replied.

"That is an admirable thing to do, but hard for those who stay at home," she said sadly, thinking how she would miss him.

Beth noticed Frank sitting on the grass, while the others played. In her shy way, she asked, "Can I do anything for you?"

"Talk to me, please. It's so dull sitting by myself," he answered.

"What do you like to talk about?"

"Cricket, boating and hunting," he said. Beth didn't know about those, but she thought hard and managed to say, "Your deer are much prettier than our ugly buffaloes." And soon they were talking about the prairies. Her sisters took great delight at the sight of their shy little sister talking to one of the *dreadful boys*.

CHAPTER THIRTEEN

Castles in the Air

Laurie was swinging in his hammock one warm afternoon. Staring up into the horse-chestnut trees, he imagined himself tossing on the ocean in a voyage around the world. Then the sound of voices brought him ashore in a flash. He looked up and there were the March girls, walking by the river. "What are they up to now?" he wondered,

running down to see. By then, they were up on the hill, Meg on her cushion, sewing, Beth making pretty things with pine cones, Amy sketching some ferns and Jo reading aloud. He felt he should go away, not being invited, but he was so lonely at home. Beth spied him and beckoned him over.

"May I join you, please?" he asked.

"Of course, but it's against the rules of the Busy Bee Society to be idle. Here, finish this story," said Jo, handing him a notebook with a story she had started.

"Tell me more about this charming and productive Society," he said eagerly.

"Mother likes us to be outside as much as possible, so we bring our work here, where we can see into the distance, to places we hope to live some day," said Jo, pointing.

Laurie looked across the wide, blue river, to the meadows beyond, far over the outskirts of the city, to the green hills that rose to meet the sky. The autumn sunset glowed, and rising high in the sky were silvery white peaks that shone.

"We imagine castles in the air and what ours would be like," said Jo.

"I have so many dreams, it would be hard to choose," said Laurie.

"Which do you like the best?" asked Meg.

"After I've seen the world, I'd like to live in Germany and be a famous musician. I'd enjoy myself, without worrying about money or business. What's yours, Meg?"

Meg started slowly, "A lovely house, full of nice food, pretty clothes, pleasant people and heaps of money."

"Why don't you say a good husband and some angelic children?" said Jo bluntly.

"I said *pleasant people*," and Meg turned to tie her shoe, so that no one could see her blushing. "You'd have nothing but horses, inkstands and novels in yours, Jo."

"A stable full of fine horses, rooms piled high with books and a magic inkstand, so my books would be as famous as Laurie's music. I want to do something heroic or wonderful that will never be forgotten."

"Mine is to stay at home with Father and Mother, and help take care of the family. With my little piano, I would be perfectly happy," said Beth.

"Mine is to go to Rome and be the best artist in the whole world," declared Amy.

"Grandfather wants me to be a tea

merchant, as he was," sighed Laurie. "But I'd travel the world tomorrow, if there was anyone else to look after him."

"Sail away and don't come home till you have seen the world," said Jo.

"That is terrible advice," said Meg. "Do your best at college, then your grandfather won't be so hard on you. As you say, there is no one else to stay with him. Do your duty and you'll get your reward, like good Mr. Brooke. He took care of his mother till she died, instead of going abroad as a tutor."

"He *is* a dear old fellow!" said Laurie.

Later that evening, remembering the conversation, Laurie thought, "I'll stay with Grandpa as long as he needs me. That is more important than any castle in the air."

CHAPTER FOURTEEN

Secrets

Jo had been writing in the attic every afternoon. She scribbled away until the last page was filled, signed her name with a flourish and threw down her pen.

"There, I've done my best!" she exclaimed, tying up the papers with a bright red ribbon. Clutching the manuscript tightly, she crept quietly downstairs. She took a bus into town and found the place she was looking for.

Several signs were swinging outside, including one for a dentist. She stood still for a moment, then walked away as rapidly as she came. She repeated this several times, then finally went in.

Sitting in a window opposite, Laurie was watching all of this with great amusement.

"Just like her to come alone to the dentist," he thought, "but if she has a bad time she'll need someone to help her home."

In ten minutes, Jo was back outside. "Laurie?" she said, surprised to see him.

"How many did you have out?" he asked.

Jo looked at her friend, puzzled. Then she began to laugh.

"What are you laughing at? You are up to some mischief, Jo," said Laurie.

"So are you. What are you doing near here?

Have you been in the billiard saloon?"

"I come and play with Ned Moffat."

"Oh dear. If you become like Ned Moffat, Mother won't let you come to our house."

"Won't she?" asked Laurie anxiously.

"She can't bear fashionable young men."

"Well, I'm not fashionable, but I do like harmless larks now and then, don't you?"

"Yes, I do, but I don't know what I'd do if you acted like Mr. King's son. He gambled, forged his father's name and got into so much trouble that he had to run away."

"Are you going to give me lectures all the way home?" asked Laurie.

"Of course not. Why?"

"Because if you're not, I'll tell you a secret. But only if you tell me yours first."

"Well," whispered Jo, "I've just left a story

with a newspaperman. He's going to tell me if he'll print it."

"Hurrah for Miss March, the celebrated American authoress!" shouted Laurie.

Jo's eyes sparkled at his belief in her.

"Now, what's your secret?" she asked.

"I saw Meg's glove in Mr. Brooke's pocket. Isn't that romantic?"

"Not if he marries her and takes her away from us!" she cried in horror.

"You'll feel better about it when somebody comes to take you away."

"I'd like to see anyone try!" said Jo.

"So would I!" said Laurie, chuckling.

Later that week, Meg caught sight of Laurie chasing Jo all over the garden. There were shrieks of laughter, a murmur of voices and a great flapping of newspaper.

"She never behaves like a young lady," sighed Meg.

In a few minutes, Jo bounced in.

"Anything interesting there?" asked Meg.

"Only a story in the paper," replied Jo.

"Read it aloud," said Amy.

"What's it called?" asked Beth.

"*The Rival Painters*," said Jo. Then taking a deep breath, she began to read, very fast. The girls listened with great interest, as it was a very romantic story.

"Who wrote it?" asked Beth.

Solemnly, Jo announced, "Your sister."

"You?" cried Meg.

"It's very good," said Amy, who especially liked the parts about the painting.

"I knew it! I knew it! Oh, Jo, I *am* proud!" And Beth ran to hug her sister.

How delighted they all were! "Well I never!" "Tell us about it." "When did it come?" "How much did you get for it?" "What *will* Father say?" cried the family and Hannah, all in one breath, as they clustered around Jo.

"Stop jabbering and I'll tell you," said Jo. "The man said he liked my story, but that he didn't pay beginners. He would print it and when I improve, anyone would pay. I shall write more and get paid for the next one. In time, I may be able to support myself and all of us."

Jo's breath gave out here, because to be independent and earn the praise of those she loved was her dearest wish.

CHAPTER FIFTEEN

A Telegram

"Nothing pleasant ever happens," said Meg one miserable November day.

"If you were in one of my books," said Jo, "I'd have some rich relation leave you a fortune unexpectedly. Then you could go abroad and return in a blaze of glory."

"People don't get left fortunes nowadays," said Meg bitterly.

"Jo and I are going to make fortunes for you all. Just see if we don't," said Amy.

Mrs. March came home and asked her usual question, "Any letter from Father?"

"Here's one of them telegram things," said Hannah, looking worried. Mrs. March read it and dropped back into her chair, as white as a sheet. Jo snatched it and read it aloud...

```
        Mrs. March:
  Your husband is very ill.
        Come at once.
  Dr. Hale, Blank Hospital,
        Washington.
```

Suddenly, the whole world seemed to change. Mrs. March stretched out her arms to her daughters and said, "I shall go at once, but it may be too late."

For several minutes there was nothing but the sound of sobbing, mingled with broken words of comfort and tears.

"Is Laurie here?" Mother said, when she had collected her thoughts.

"He is and ready to do anything you need, Ma'am," Laurie said promptly.

"Would you send a telegram saying I will come at once and then tell Aunt March? And Jo, would you fetch a few supplies for me?"

Jo knew that Mother would have to borrow money for her journey and wondered what she could do to help.

Laurie came back from Aunt March's with some money and a note saying she knew no good would come of Father going to war.

By now, it was getting dark and Jo had still not returned. Laurie went off to find her. But just after he left, she came walking in with several packages, her expression a mixture of satisfaction and regret, which puzzled the family as much as the sum of money she handed to Mother.

"That's my contribution to bring Father home!" she said.

"My dear, where did you get it? I hope you haven't done anything rash?" said Mother.

"I only sold what was my own." And as she spoke, Jo took off her bonnet. Her long chestnut hair was cut short.

"My dear girl, you didn't need to do this," said Mother.

"She doesn't look like Jo any more, but I love her for it!" said Beth.

"It's cool and light. The barber said it will soon grow into a boyish crop that will be easy to keep tidy. I don't think I shall ever have it long again," she said, trying to look

as if she liked it. But she didn't fool anyone.

"What made you do it?" asked Amy, who would never dream of cutting off her hair.

"I wanted to do something for Father," replied Jo. "In a barber's window, I saw wigs of hair with the prices marked on. So I asked what he would give for mine. He did seem surprised at first, but when I told him why, his wife said kindly, *Take it, Thomas. I'd do as much for our Jimmy if I had hair worth selling.*"

"Who was Jimmy?" asked Amy.

"Her son in the army," replied Jo.

"Didn't you feel dreadful when the first cut came?" asked Meg, with a shiver.

"I took one last look at my hair and that was the end of it," said Jo.

Later that evening, the conversation turned to Father and the happy times they would have when he finally came home.

"Let's go to bed now, for we must be up early," said Mrs. March. "We need all the sleep we can get. Good night, my darlings."

Meg thought Jo was asleep, until a stifled sob made her exclaim, "Jo, dear, are you crying about Father?"

"No. My... my hair!" burst out Jo. "Please don't tell anyone I'm upset about it. I thought you were asleep."

"I can't sleep. I'm so anxious," said Meg.

"Try to think about something pleasant and you'll soon drop off," comforted Jo.

Meg thought about Mr. Brooke's handsome brown eyes and in no time, she was fast asleep, dreaming of her castle in the air.

CHAPTER SIXTEEN

Mother Leaves

Breakfast at such an early hour seemed odd. "Meg, watch over your sisters while I'm away," said Mother. "Ask Hannah for help if you need to, or go to Mr. Laurence. Jo, write to me often and don't do anything rash. Beth, keep up your housework, and Amy, do as you're told and help all you can."

"We will, Mother! We will!" they promised.

As the carriage approached, the girls kissed their mother and sent loving messages to Father. Mr. Brooke had agreed to accompany Mrs. March to Washington, and Laurie and his grandfather came to see them off.

The girls could not help crying as the carriage rolled away. Hannah came to the rescue, armed with a coffeepot.

"My dear young ladies, remember what your mother said. We'll have a cup of coffee, then let's get to work and be a credit to the family."

"I shall go to Aunt March as usual," said Jo.

"I shall go to the Kings, though I'd much rather stay at home and help here," said Meg.

"No need for that. Beth and I can keep house perfectly well," put in Amy, feeling grown-up.

As Meg and Jo left for work, they looked back

at the window where Mother used to wave to them. There was Beth in her place, smiling and waving.

"That is just like sweet Beth," said Jo.

Every day, Mr. Brooke sent a bulletin from Washington, and as the head of the family, Meg insisted on reading them out. The letters grew more cheerful as the weeks passed and Father's health improved.

CHAPTER SEVENTEEN

Faithful Little Beth

Everyone worked hard. But after hearing the good news about Father, they slipped back into their old ways. Only Beth faithfully carried out her duties.

"I have been to see the Hummels every day this week. Will you go today, Meg?" she asked.

Meg promised she would go tomorrow.

"I'd go but I want to finish my writing,"

said Jo. "You go today, Beth."

"My head aches and I'm tired," said Beth.

"Amy will be in soon. She'll go," said Meg.

An hour passed and Amy did not come. Beth quietly put on her coat, filled her basket with odds and ends for the poor children and went out into the chilly air. It was late when she came back. Jo found her shivering by the medicine cabinet.

"What's the matter?" asked Jo.

"Mrs. Hummel's baby died of scarlet fever. I was with it every day, so the doctor said I should take belladonna, or I'd get it. Don't come near me or you'll get it too," said Beth, holding out her hand to keep Jo away.

"I've had it before, so I can't get it again," said Jo, "but it would serve me right if I did, for letting you go."

Hannah came and felt Beth's head, saying, "You have a fever. We'll get Dr. Bangs."

Dr. Bangs came and confirmed the dreadful news that Beth did indeed have scarlet fever.

"Jo, stay and look after Beth," said Hannah. "Amy has never had it, so she must go to stay with Aunt March, out of the way."

"I'll go and tell her," said Meg.

"I'd rather have the fever than go to Aunt March!" Amy declared. Laurie found her sobbing and quickly came up with a plan.

"If you go to Aunt March's, I'll come and take you out every day. Won't that be better than moping here?" he offered.

"Every single day?" asked Amy.

"See if I don't!"

"*And* take me to see plays?"

"Dozens of 'em!"

"Well, I guess I will go," said Amy slowly.

So off they went to Aunt March's.

"No more than I expected, if you will go poking about among poor folks," was Aunt March's reaction. "Amy can stay, if she makes herself useful. Don't cry, child."

Amy was on the point of crying, but Laurie pulled the parrot's tail, which made Polly call out, "Bless my boots!" so she laughed instead.

"Hold your tongue, you disrespectful old bird!" said Aunt March.

"Hold your tongue, you disrespectful old bird!" cried Polly back.

"I don't think I can bear this, but I will have to try," thought Amy, as Laurie left.

"You old fright!" screamed Polly and at that Amy couldn't hold back a tiny sniff.

CHAPTER EIGHTEEN

Dark Days

Jo stayed with Beth day and night, while Meg helped Hannah. Beth's fever grew worse and she started calling out for Mother. Jo grew really frightened. Meg begged Hannah to write to Mother, but Hannah thought this would only make her worry, since she would not be able to leave Father and come home.

How dark the days seemed, as if a shadow

hovered over the once happy home.

Beth's beloved doll, Joanna, lay beside her. She wanted her cats too, but she was worried they would get sick. She sent loving messages to Amy, and asked Jo to write to Mother and Father, so they would not think she had forgotten them. Often she lay for hours, tossing to and fro in a fever.

When Dr. Bangs visited, one winter day, he looked at her, then said to Hannah, "If Mrs. March *can* leave her husband, I think she should come home."

Hannah nodded solemnly. Jo wrote a telegram to Mother and rushed out to send it. As she returned, Laurie came in. Seeing the misery on Jo's face, he asked quickly, "Is Beth much worse?"

"She doesn't look like Beth anymore. I've

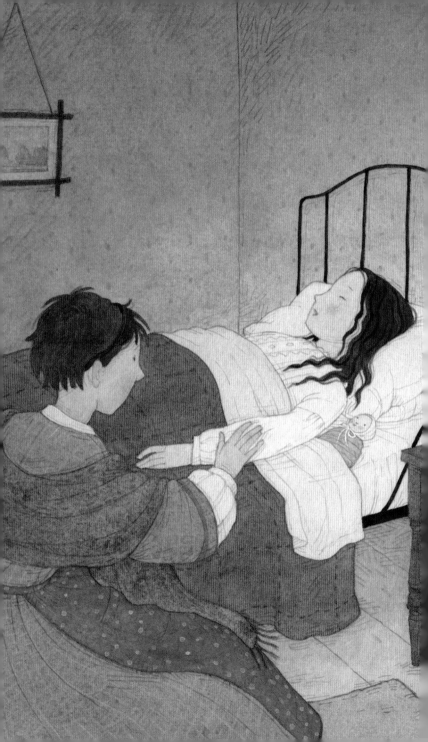

sent for Mother, but she may be too late," said Jo, tears streaming down her cheeks.

"I telegraphed your mother yesterday," he said. "Grandpa and I thought she would never forgive us if anything happened to Beth. Her train will arrive late tonight. I shall go and fetch her."

"Oh, Laurie, how can I ever thank you?" sobbed Jo.

Beth lay in bed all day, pale and weak, only now and then muttering, "Water!" But everything appeared more hopeful now that Mother was on her way.

By evening, Hannah lay on the sofa and fell fast asleep. Mr. Laurence stayed with them, worrying how Mrs. March would feel when she arrived. Laurie lay on the rug and stared into the fire, looking thoughtful.

Meg and Jo never forgot that night and how powerless they felt. Both watched Beth and noticed a change. Her beloved little face looked so pale and peaceful now. The look of pain had gone. Jo leaned low over her dear sister and kissed her damp forehead.

Hannah awoke from her sleep and hurried over to the bed. She looked at Beth, felt her hands and exclaimed, "The fever's turned! She's getting better."

Before the girls could believe it, Dr. Bangs came to confirm it. He said, with a fatherly look, "Yes, my dears, I think the little girl will pull through this time. Keep the house quiet, let her sleep and when she wakes, give her—"

What they were to give, Meg and Jo never heard, for both crept into the dark hall and, sitting on the stairs, held each other close, their hearts too full for words. When they went back, they found Beth breathing quietly, as if she had just fallen asleep.

"If Mother would only come now!" said Jo.

They looked out of the window at the snow falling softly.

"Listen!" cried Jo.

There was a sound of bells at the door, a cry from Hannah and then Laurie's voice, "Girls, she's here! She's here!"

CHAPTER NINETEEN

Amy's Will

Amy was having a hard time following Aunt March's strict rules. Laurie took her out every day and they had a splendid time, but Aunt March expected her to clean and dust, as well as do her schoolwork. In the afternoons, she liked Amy to read to her. And the evenings were even worse, as Aunt March told long stories about her youth, which were so dull, Amy was always ready to go to bed.

If it had not been for Esther, the maid, Amy felt she could not have got through that terrible time. Esther allowed her to roam the great house and examine all the curious things stored in ancient wardrobes and chests. One cabinet was filled with shimmering jewels: garnets, diamonds, pearls, Aunt March's wedding ring, Uncle March's watch and rings of gleaming black jet.

"Which would you choose?" asked Esther.

"I like diamonds best, but I'd like them in a necklace," she said. She picked up a string of gold and ebony beads, with a heavy cross hanging from them.

"I do like this necklace," she said.

"That is a rosary. People use them when they say their prayers," said Esther.

"You seem to take a great deal of comfort in your prayers, Esther. I wish I could."

"I can make the dressing room into a small chapel for you, if you like, so you can pray there," suggested Esther.

Amy liked the idea. Being away from home was lonely and she thought it might help.

"What do you think will happen to all these pretty things when Aunt March dies?" she asked, gently replacing the shining rosary.

"They will go to you and your sisters," said Esther. "I witnessed Madame's will."

"How nice!" said Amy.

"I believe that turquoise ring will be given to you, as Madame likes your good manners."

"Oh, I'll be a lamb, if I can have that lovely ring! It's much prettier than Kitty Bryant's. I do like Aunt March after all," said Amy.

Esther put a little table in the dressing room and, above it, hung a painting of Mary holding baby Jesus. Every day, Amy sat alone to think quietly and say prayers for Beth. She did her best to be good, even though no one saw her or praised her for it.

She decided she should write a will, so that if she died, her treasures could be divided fairly. She wrote it out, with Esther's help on the legal terms. Esther signed it as her witness, and Amy left a space for Laurie to sign it too.

One rainy day, when she was trying on an old-fashioned dress of Aunt March's, complete with a pink turban, she was so busy parading up and down in front of the mirror, that she didn't see Laurie at the door. As he told Jo later, it was a comical sight, with Polly imitating her and exclaiming, "Ain't we fine? Ha! Ha!"

When she saw Laurie, she handed him a piece of paper and said, "I want to consult you about a serious matter. Please can you tell me if this is legal."

Laurie read the will, doing his best not to laugh at her funny spelling:

MY WILL AND TESTIMENT
I, Amy Curtis March, being in sane mind, bequeethe all my earthly proputty – namely:
To my father, my best works of art.
To my mother, all my clothes, except the blue apron. Also my self-portrait, with much love.
To my dear sister Meg, my turkquoise ring (if I get it) and my sketch of her.
To Jo, my bronze inkstand – she lost the cover – and my most preshus plaster rabbit, because I am sorry I burned up her stories.
To Beth, my dolls, my fan and my regret that

I made fun of dear old Joanna.

To my friend Theodore Laurence, any of my artistic works he chewses.

To Mr. Laurence, my purple box to thank him for looking after us all, but espeshilly Beth.

To my best friend Kitty Bryant, the blue silk apron and my gold bead ring.

To Hannah, all my patchwork.

To this will and testiment, I set my hand and seal this 20th day of Nov. Anno Domino 1861.

Amy Curtis March

Witnesses: Esther Valnor and ....

Amy asked Laurie to sign his name.

"What gave you this idea? Did you know that Beth has given away her things?" asked Laurie, as he was signing.

She explained, then said worriedly, "What about Beth?"

"She felt so ill that she told Jo she wanted to give her piano to Meg, her cats to you and poor old Joanna to Jo, who she knew would look after her. She left locks of hair to the rest of us. She never thought of a will."

Amy thought for a moment, then said, "Please add that I wish *all* my curls to be cut off and given to my friends, even though it will spoil my looks."

Laurie added it, smiling at Amy's last and greatest sacrifice. Then she whispered, "Is there really any danger about Beth?"

"She is much better now, but we must all look after her," he said, putting a comforting arm around her.

Amy went to her chapel to pray, feeling that a million turquoise rings would not comfort her if she ever lost her shy, gentle sister.

CHAPTER TWENTY

Confiding in Mother

Amy cried with joy when Mother came to see her. She showed her the little chapel.

"When I get home, I would like to have a place to pray, where I can put the painting I copied," she said.

As she pointed to the picture on the wall, Mrs. March saw something blue glinting on Amy's finger.

"I wanted to speak to you about this," said Amy. "Aunt gave me this today, because she said I am a credit to her. Please can I wear it?"

"It is pretty, but you're too young to wear a ring, Amy," said Mrs. March.

"I want to wear it to remind me not to be selfish," said Amy, so earnestly that her mother listened carefully now. "Beth isn't selfish and that's why everyone loves her. I'm going to try to be more like Beth and this ring would remind me."

"Wear your ring, dear, and do your best. Now I must go back to Beth, but we will have you home again soon."

That evening, Jo slipped upstairs and found Mother. She stood a minute twisting her fingers in her hair, with a worried look.

"What is it, dear?" asked Mrs. March.

"I want to tell you something, Marmee."

"About Meg?"

"You guessed! Laurie told me that Mr. Brooke admitted he loves her."

"Do you think Meg loves him?"

"I don't know anything about love and nonsense like that!" cried Jo. "In books, girls blush, faint and act like fools. Meg doesn't do anything of the sort. She only blushes a little when Laurie jokes about love."

"So you think Meg is not interested in John then?" asked Mother.

"Who?" cried Jo.

"I call Mr. Brooke *John* now, since spending time with him at the hospital."

"Oh dear! I knew you'd take his side."

"John has been so kind to poor Father that we couldn't help getting fond of him. He has told us he loves Meg, but he wants to earn a good living before asking her to marry him."

"This is worse than I imagined!"

"Jo, don't say anything to Meg yet. This is our secret. I want to see for myself whether she loves him or not when he returns."

"She'll see those handsome brown eyes she talks about so much, and her heart will melt like butter in the sun. And that will be the end of our fun times together!"

Mrs. March sighed.

"It is natural you should all go to homes of your own in time, but Meg is only seventeen. Your father and I have agreed she should not be married before she is twenty. If she and John love one another, they can wait."

"Wouldn't you rather she married someone rich?" asked Jo.

"With John, Meg will have the love of a good man and that is worth far more than any fortune. I know from my own experience how much genuine happiness can be had in a plain, little house."

Meg came in and showed Mother a letter she had written to Father.

"Beautifully written, dear. Please add that I send my love to John," said Mrs. March.

"Do you call him *John?*" asked Meg, smiling and looking into her mother's eyes.

"I do. He's been like a son to us," replied Mrs. March.

"I'm glad of that. Good night, Mother. It is so comforting to have you here."

As Meg went away, Mrs. March thought to herself, "Meg does not love John yet, but I think she will."

CHAPTER TWENTY-ONE

Laurie Makes Mischief

Jo did her best to keep the secret, but it wasn't easy with Laurie trying to tease it out of her. In the end, he guessed it had something to do with Meg and Mr. Brooke.

One day, when Jo handed Meg a note from the post office, Meg let out a frightened cry.

"What is it?" said Mother, running to her.

"John didn't send me this note!" she said,

pulling a crumpled piece of paper from her pocket. "You did, Jo! You and Laurie wrote it. How could you be so cruel?"

"I did not!" cried Jo, grasping the note and reading it out loud...

My Dearest Meg,

I can no longer hide my love for you. I think your parents would approve. My dear, sweet girl, send me, through Laurie, one word that you like me too,

Your devoted John

"I'd have done a better job than that and written something sensible!" said Jo. "Mr. Brooke would never write stuff like that."

"But it looks like his writing," faltered Meg.

"Oh, Meg, you didn't answer it, did you?" cried Mrs. March.

"Yes, I did!" and Meg hid her face in shame.

"Tell me the whole story," said Mother.

"I received the first note," began Meg. "I didn't think you'd mind if I kept the secret for a few days, while I decided what to say."

"And what did you say?" asked Mrs. March.

"That I'm too young and don't wish to have any secrets from you. I would like to be his friend, but nothing more for a long time."

Mrs. March smiled, pleased with her daughter's sensible response.

"How did he reply?" asked Jo.

"He's just said he never sent me a love letter!" cried Meg, in despair.

Jo looked closely at the note that had just arrived and then the crumpled one.

"I don't believe Brooke wrote either note. Laurie wrote them both," she said, realizing

this was his way of finding out the secret.

"Jo, please bring Laurie here, so I can get to the bottom of this," said Mother.

While Jo was getting Laurie, Mrs. March gently told Meg of Mr. Brooke's real feelings.

"Do you love him enough to wait until he can make a home for you?" she asked.

"I've been so worried, Marmee, I don't want to have anything to do with love for a long time," answered Meg. "If John doesn't know anything about this, please don't tell him. I won't be made a fool of!"

Mrs. March promised to keep silent.

When Laurie arrived, Meg and Jo left the room, so Mrs. March could face the culprit alone. They never knew what was said in that room, but when they were called back in, Laurie looked deeply ashamed.

"I'm sorry, Meg. I promise never to tell him until my dying day," he swore, and Meg forgave him.

Later, Jo went over to see Laurie and found him fuming in his room.

"I can't bear it!" he growled. "Grandpa wants me to tell him what your mother wanted me for, but I can't without mentioning Meg. I won't go down until he says sorry for not trusting me!"

"You can't stay here," said Jo.

"I don't intend to. I'll go to Washington to see Brooke. When Grandpa misses me he'll come around fast enough."

"I wish I could run off, too," said Jo.

"Come on, then! Why not?"

"Don't tempt me, Laurie," she said, longing for adventure.

Instead, she went to find old Mr. Laurence.

"Come in!" came a gruff voice.

"I'm here to return a book, Sir," she began.

"Want any more?" he asked.

"Yes, please. I'd like the second volume."

He pushed the library steps towards her and she skipped to the top. Mr Laurence then spoke abruptly, "What has that boy been up to? I know he's been up to some mischief."

"He has, but we have forgiven him."

"If he's done anything wrong, he must confess and be punished. Out with it, Jo."

Jo was perched at the top of steps and he was at the bottom, so she had no escape.

"Mother asked us not to tell, as that would make trouble for someone else."

"If you give me your word he is keeping the secret for someone else, I'll forgive him,"

he said, looking relieved. "Bring him down."

"He won't come, Sir, because you didn't believe him. He is talking about going to Washington. A formal apology will make him see how foolish he is being. I can take it up to him, if you like."

Mr. Laurence said, "You're a smart girl, Jo. Here, give me some paper."

Jo slipped the apology under Laurie's door. A minute later, he bounded downstairs, back in good spirits, saying, "What a good fellow you are, Jo!"

Everyone thought the matter was over, but it wasn't for Meg. She never spoke about Mr. Brooke to anyone, but she thought – and dreamed – about him a lot.

CHAPTER TWENTY-TWO

Pleasant Days

Christmas morning dawned and they all gathered in the drawing room. Laurie brought in the gifts and Jo made funny speeches as she presented them.

"I'm so full of happiness that if Father was here, I think I'd burst," said Beth, as Jo carried her to the study to rest. Mrs. March agreed, as she looked at the smiling faces around her.

Just then, Laurie opened the door and said

in a breathless voice, "Here's another Christmas present for the March family."

Before the words were fully out, a tall man appeared, leaning on the arm of another tall man. Of course, there was a general stampede and Mr. March became invisible in the embrace of four pairs of loving arms. Jo nearly fainted. Mr. Brooke kissed Meg entirely by mistake, as he tried to explain to her later. And Amy, usually so dignified, tumbled over a stool, and didn't bother to get up, but hugged her father's legs. Filled with joy, Mrs. March warned, "Hush! Remember Beth."

But it was too late. The door flew open and Beth ran straight into her father's arms.

Mr. March told them how kind Mr. Brooke had been. Mrs. March smiled and asked if Mr. Brooke would like to have something to eat.

They all sat down for Christmas dinner. Hannah brought in the fat turkey, browned and decorated, and the plum pudding melted in their mouths. Old Mr. Laurence and Laurie joined them and everyone told stories, sang songs and had a thoroughly good time.

As the guests departed, the happy family sat together around the fire.

"Just a year ago we were groaning over the dismal Christmas we expected to have. Do you remember?" asked Jo.

"It's been a very pleasant year," said Meg, smiling into the fire, thinking of Mr. Brooke.

"I think it's been a pretty hard one," said Amy, looking thoughtfully at her ring.

"I'm glad it's over, because we've got you back," whispered Beth to Father.

"I am pleased to see you are all developing

into admirable young women," said Mr. March. Taking up Meg's hand, he said, "I remember when this hand was pale and smooth, but these blemishes show me you have been working hard, at the expense of your vanity."

"What about Jo? She has tried so hard and been so good to me," said Beth.

"In spite of the curly crop," said Mr. March, "I see a young lady who does not talk slang as she used to, but takes care of a certain little person in such a kind and gentle way. I miss my wild girl, but I am more than satisfied to get this strong, helpful woman in her place."

"Now, Beth," said Amy, longing for her turn, but ready to wait.

"She is not as shy as she used to be," he began cheerfully. But remembering how he had so nearly lost her, he held her close and said tenderly, "I've got you safe now, Beth, and that's how I'll keep you."

Next he looked at Amy and said, "I noticed that Amy ran errands for her mother all afternoon and patiently looks after everyone. She has not even mentioned a very pretty ring which she wears, so I believe she has learned to think of other people more than herself. She has a great talent for art, but also a talent for making life beautiful for others."

Beth slipped out of her father's arms and went to her little piano. Softly, she touched the keys and sang carols in the sweet voice they had thought they would never hear again.

CHAPTER TWENTY-THREE

Aunt March Settles the Question

"I bet if John asked you to marry him, you'd cry or blush, instead of giving a good, decided *no*," said Jo to Meg, the next day.

"I am not as weak as you think," replied Meg. "I would tell him quite calmly, *Thank you, Mr. Brooke, but I agree with Father and Mother that I am too young to get engaged.*"

There was a tap at the door and it *was* Mr.

Brooke. Jo slipped out to give Meg a chance to make her dignified speech. But instead Meg just mumbled, "I'll get Mother."

"Don't go. Are you afraid of me?" he asked.

She put out her hand to him and said gratefully, "How can I be, when you have been so kind to Father?"

He looked at her with so much love in his brown eyes, that her heart began to flutter.

"Do you care for me?" he asked. "I love you so much. Please tell me."

This was the moment for her calm speech, but Meg forgot every single word and instead answered shyly, "I don't know."

At that moment, Aunt March came hobbling in, looking for Father. Meg looked as if she'd seen a ghost and Mr. Brooke fled to the study.

"What's going on here?" thundered the old

lady. "Is that Brooke, the boy's tutor? I have heard all about this. I suspect he wants to marry you because you have rich relations!"

"How dare you say that! John is good and kind, and we are both willing to work hard," said Meg, glad to defend John. "I know I'll be happy with him because he loves me and I..."

Meg stopped there, remembering all of a sudden that he might be overhearing her.

"Well, if you do marry him, don't expect a penny of my money!" cried Aunt March, slamming the door as she left.

Mr. Brooke came in and said, all in one breath, "I couldn't help hearing, Meg. Thank *you* for defending me, and Aunt March for proving that you do care for me a little bit."

"I didn't know how much," began Meg.

"May I marry you, my dear?" he asked her.

Here was another chance to make her speech, but Meg just whispered, "Yes, John."

Jo came downstairs, and hearing no sound at the door, thought, "She has given her speech after all. I'll go in and we'll have a good laugh about it."

But poor Jo never got her laugh, for there he was on the sofa, with her sister on his knee.

"Congratulate us, we're engaged!" he said.

That was too much for Jo and she rushed out to tell the family the terrible news.

Beth and Amy were thrilled, while Mr. and Mrs. March went straight into the drawing room. They looked very impressed when John told them his plans for his life with Meg.

"You can't say nothing pleasant ever happens now, can you, Meg?" said Amy.

"I can't. How much has happened since I said

that!" answered Meg, in a blissful dream.

"What a year this has been, but it ends well, after all," said Mrs. March.

The front door banged and in came Laurie. On hearing the news, he was full of congratulations for Meg and Mr. Brooke.

"Thank you. I invite you to our wedding on the spot," answered Mr. Brooke happily.

"I'll come to see Jo's face alone," said Laurie.

"I wish things could stay as they are," said Jo to Laurie, with a little quiver in her voice. "I'm losing my dearest friend in Meg."

"Cheer up. You still have me," said Laurie. "Don't you wish we could see into the future?"

"No," said Jo, smiling as she looked around the room. "I might see something sad and I don't believe any of us could be happier than we are this very minute."

Edited by Lesley Sims
Designed by Lenka Jones

Series Designer: Russell Punter